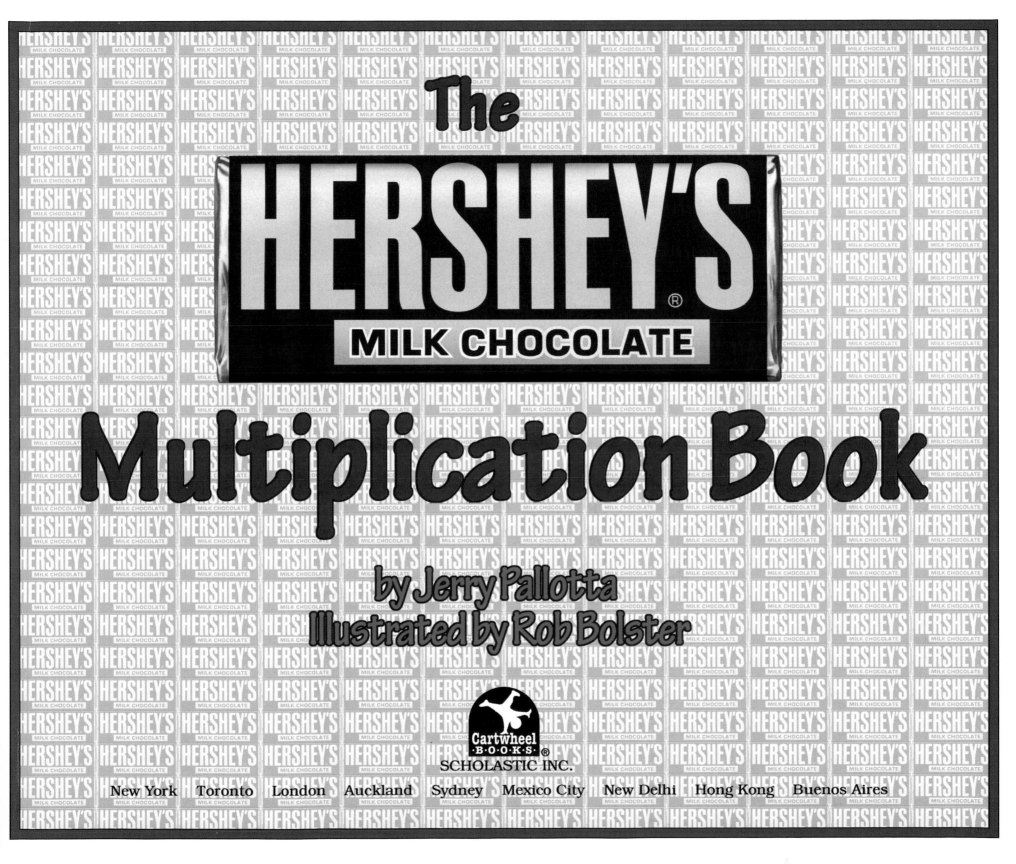

The HERSHEY'S MILK CHOCOLATE
Multiplication Book

by Jerry Pallotta
Illustrated by Rob Bolster

Cartwheel BOOKS®
SCHOLASTIC INC.

New York   Toronto   London   Auckland   Sydney   Mexico City   New Delhi   Hong Kong   Buenos Aires

Extra special thanks to Henry Quinlan and Boston College High School.

—— *Jerry Pallotta*

This book is dedicated to Diana Hampe, one of the best art teachers I know.

—— *Rob Bolster*

Library of Congress Cataloging-in-Publication Data
Pallotta, Jerry.
    The Hershey's milk chocolate multiplication book / by Jerry Pallotta; illustrated by Rob Bolster.
        p. cm.
    ISBN 0-439-23623-1(pob.) – ISBN 0-439-25412-4(pbk.)
    1. Multiplication–Juvenile literature [1.Multiplication.] I. Bolster, Rob, ill. II. Title.

QA115.P245 2002
513.2'13–de21

2001020577

10 9 8 7 6 5 4 3 2 1   02 03 04 05 06

Printed in Mexico   **49**
This edition first printing, February 2002

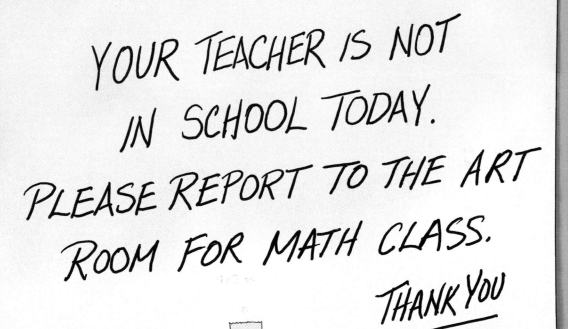

Milk Chocolate times math equals art.

Count the sections of this HERSHEY'S® milk chocolate bar. One, two, three, four, five, six, seven, eight, nine, ten, eleven, and twelve. You did it, but there is an easier way! It is called multiplication.

This is a grid. Inside is an array of numbers. An array is a set of numbers arranged in order. Look for patterns.

	1	2	3	4	5	6	7	8	9	10	11	12	13	14	15
1	1	2	3	4	5	6	7	8	9	10	11	12	13	14	15
2	2	4	6	8	10	12	14	16	18	20	22	24	26	28	30
3	3	6	9	12	15	18	21	24	27	30	33	36	39	42	45
4	4	8	12	16	20	24	28	32	36	40	44	48	52	56	60
5	5	10	15	20	25	30	35	40	45	50	55	60	65	70	75
6	6	12	18	24	30	36	42	48	54	60	66	72	78	84	90
7	7	14	21	28	35	42	49	56	63	70	77	84	91	98	105
8	8	16	24	32	40	48	56	64	72	80	88	96	104	112	120
9	9	18	27	36	45	54	63	72	81	90	99	108	117	126	135
10	10	20	30	40	50	60	70	80	90	100	110	120	130	140	150

In math, this is a multiplication sign, or a times sign. It is used to multiply numbers.

Here is an equals sign. It is used in equations to show that two or more numbers are equal in value.

$$3 \times 4 = 12$$

The HERSHEY'S milk chocolate bar is perfect to use when learning multiplication. This candy bar has three sections in each vertical column and four sections in each horizontal row. Three times four equals twelve. We did not have to count every one of the sections. We multiplied. In the art room, the kids are drawing lines with pen and colored ink.

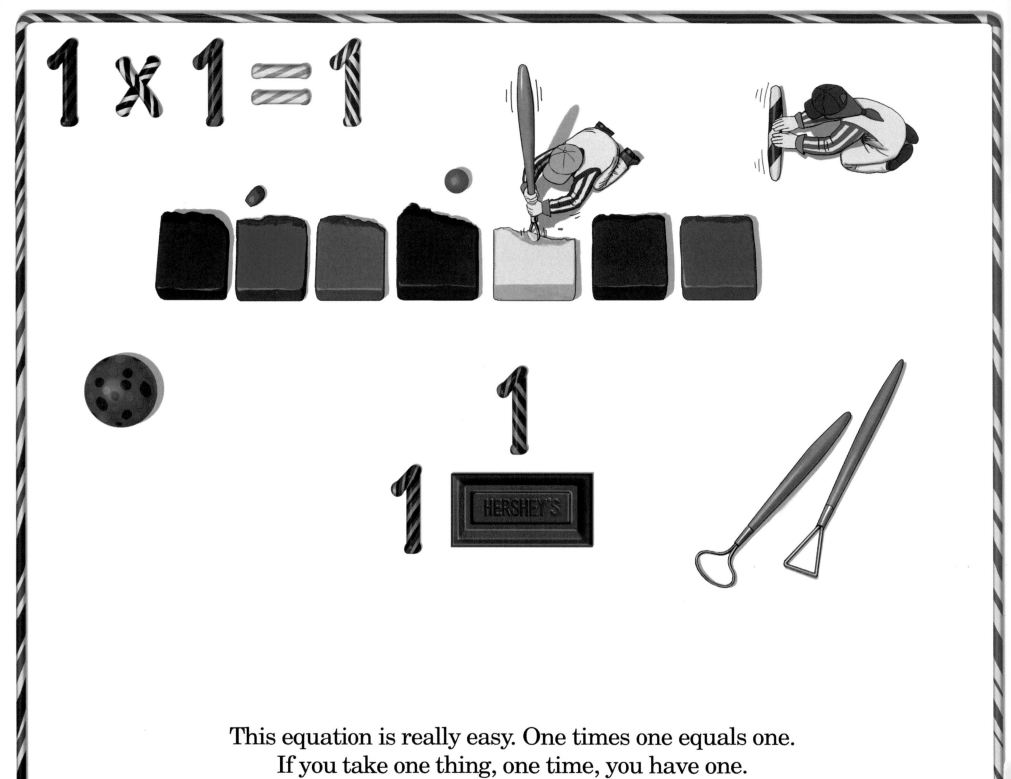

This equation is really easy. One times one equals one.
If you take one thing, one time, you have one.
Sculptures and shapes can be made with clay. Shape it, knead it, roll it, squeeze it.

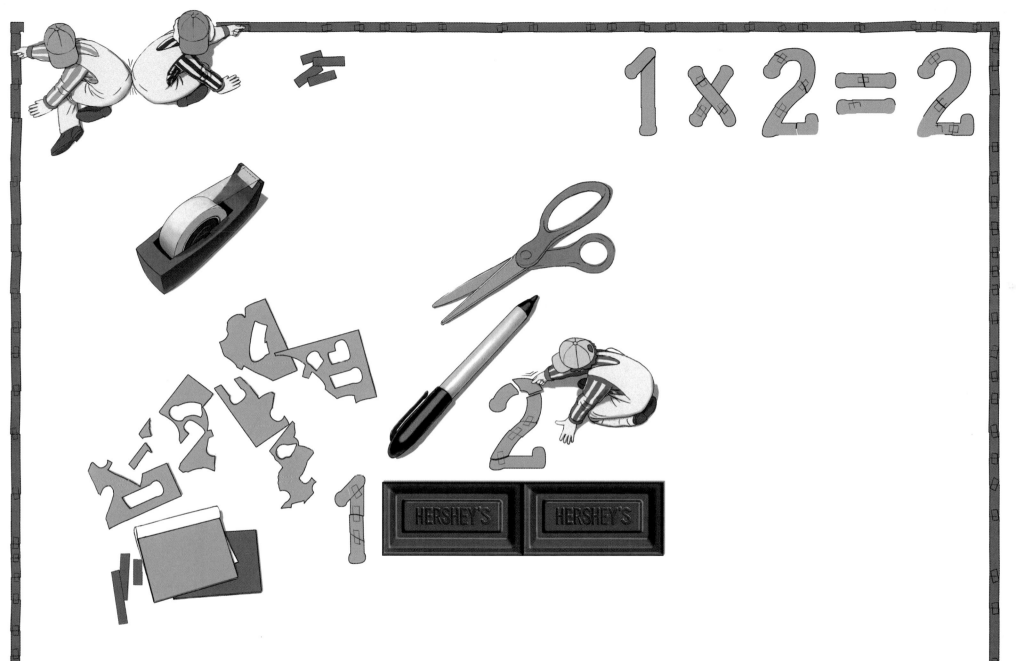

If you take one thing, two times, you have two! One times two equals two.
The kids are using scissors, tape, and colored paper to make cutouts of the numbers.

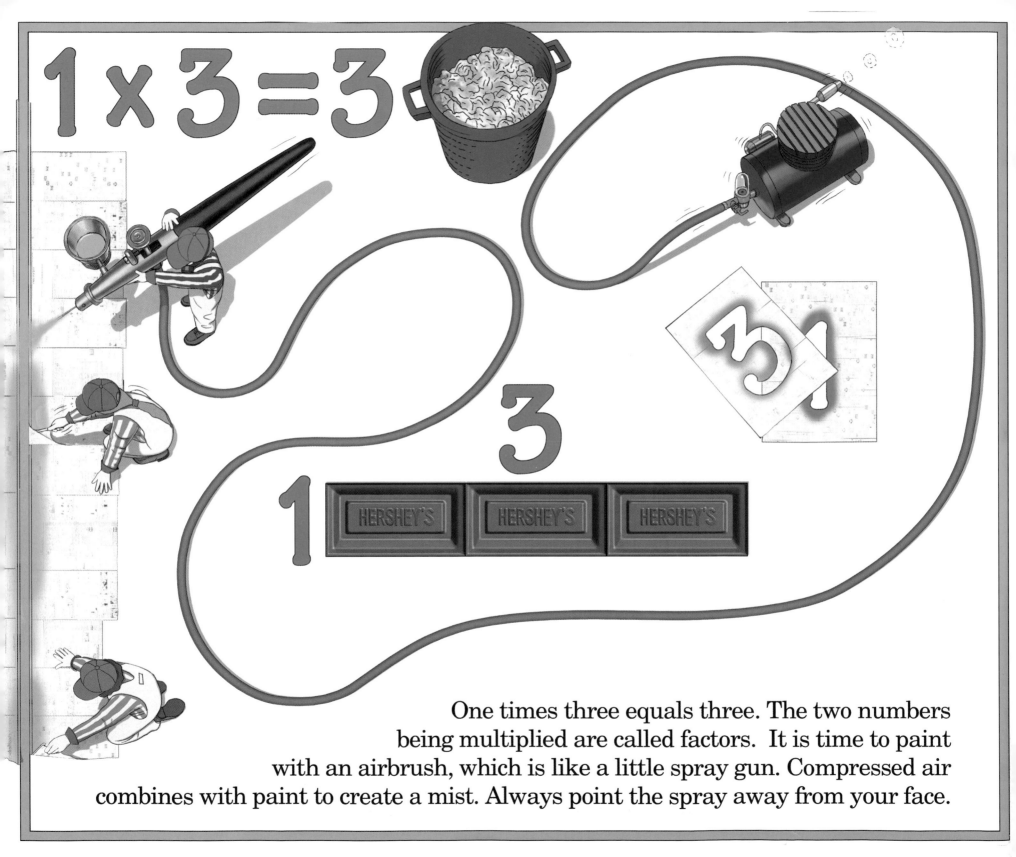

1 × 3 = 3

One times three equals three. The two numbers being multiplied are called factors. It is time to paint with an airbrush, which is like a little spray gun. Compressed air combines with paint to create a mist. Always point the spray away from your face.

$$1 \times 4 = 4$$

One times four equals four. When doing multiplication, the answer is called the product. A factor times a factor equals a product.
Hey kids, be careful with the paints. Don't forget to clean your brushes.

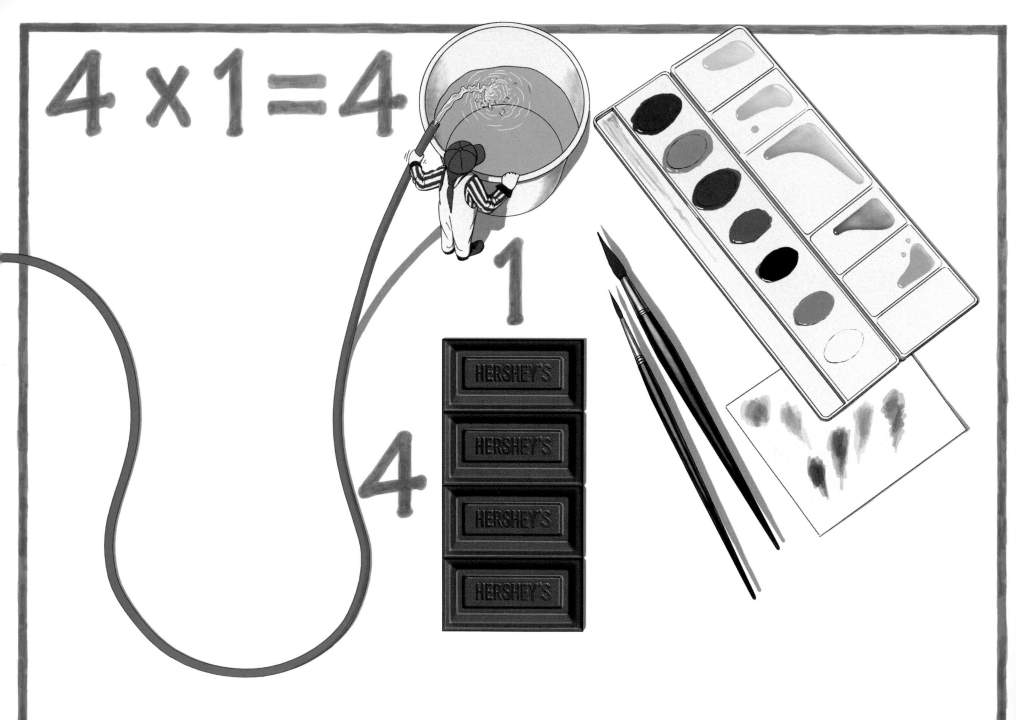

With watercolors, the kids have painted a horizontal equation.
This equation goes from side to side just like the horizon. Four times one equals four.
That cup is not a swimming pool—do not dive in!

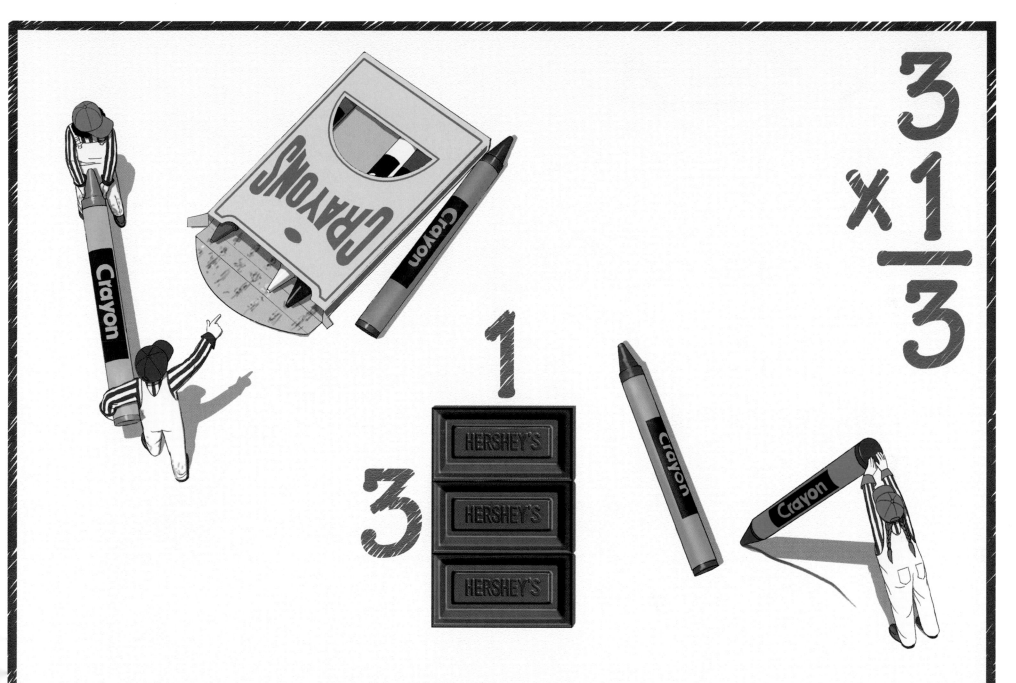

This page is a little different. The kids have colored a vertical equation using crayons. This multiplication fact goes up and down instead of across. Three times one equals three.

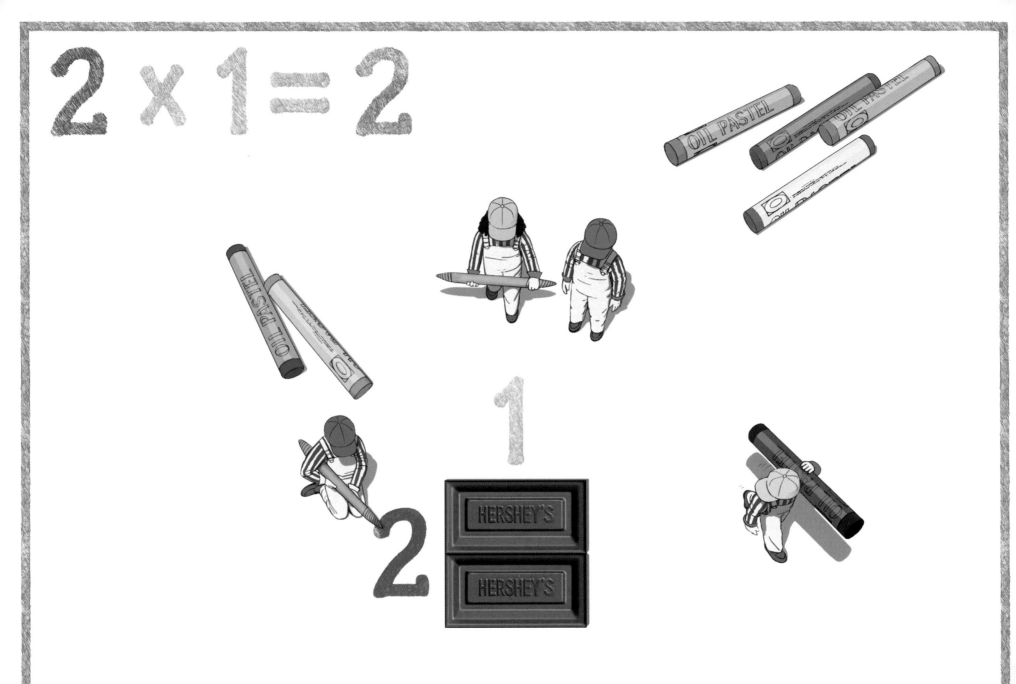

2 × 1 = 2

Numbers can be multiplied in any order. If the two factors are reversed, the product is the same. Two times one equals two. One times two equals two. This is called the commutative property of multiplication. For a lighter, softer color, you can draw with pastels.

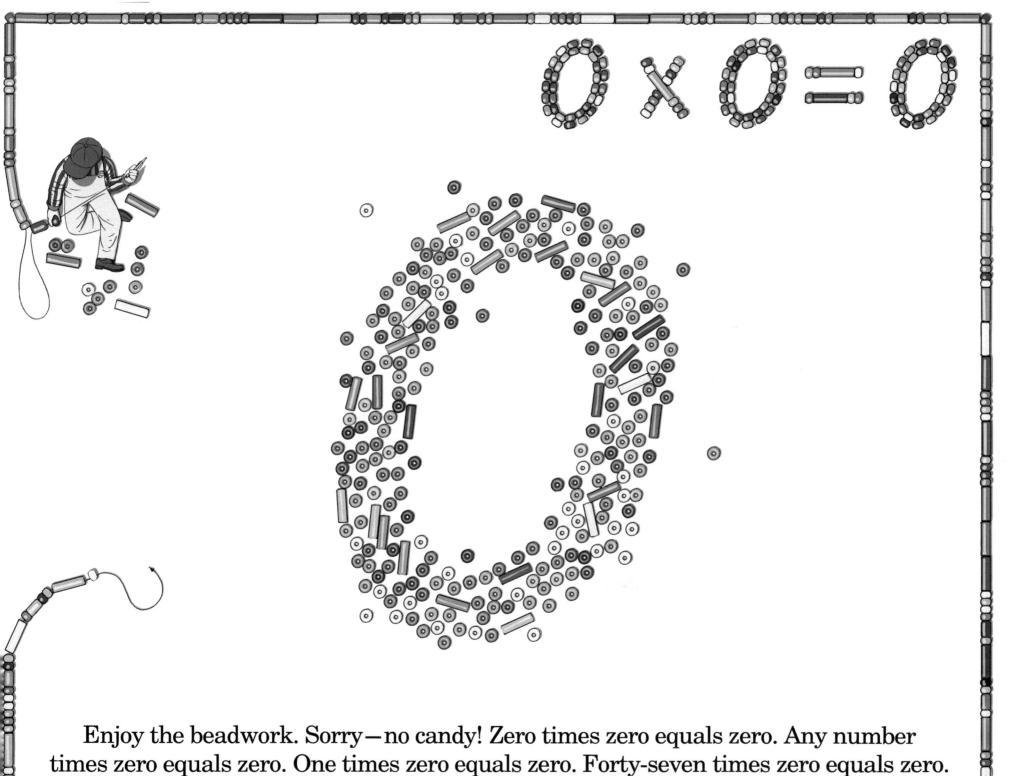

$$0 \times 0 = 0$$

Enjoy the beadwork. Sorry—no candy! Zero times zero equals zero. Any number times zero equals zero. One times zero equals zero. Forty-seven times zero equals zero. One zillion times zero equals zero. Zero is an important number, but it has no value.

0x0=0	0x1=0	0x2=0	0x3=0	0x4=0	0x5=0
1x0=0	1x1=1	1x2=2	1x3=3	1x4=4	1x5=5
2x0=0	2x1=2	2x2=4	2x3=6	2x4=8	2x5=10
3x0=0	3x1=3	3x2=6	3x3=9	3x4=12	3x5=15
4x0=0	4x1=4	4x2=8	4x3=12	4x4=16	4x5=20
5x0=0	5x1=5	5x2=10	5x3=15	5x4=20	5x5=25
6x0=0	6x1=6	6x2=12	6x3=18	6x4=24	6x5=30
7x0=0	7x1=7	7x2=14	7x3=21	7x4=28	7x5=35
8x0=0	8x1=8	8x2=16	8x3=24	8x4=32	8x5=40
9x0=0	9x1=9	9x2=18	9x3=27	9x4=36	9x5=45
10x0=0	10x1=10	10x2=20	10x3=30	10x4=40	10x5=50

Basic Multiplication Facts

$0 \times 6 = 0$	$0 \times 7 = 0$	$0 \times 8 = 0$	$0 \times 9 = 0$	$0 \times 10 = 0$
$1 \times 6 = 6$	$1 \times 7 = 7$	$1 \times 8 = 8$	$1 \times 9 = 9$	$1 \times 10 = 10$
$2 \times 6 = 12$	$2 \times 7 = 14$	$2 \times 8 = 16$	$2 \times 9 = 18$	$2 \times 10 = 20$
$3 \times 6 = 18$	$3 \times 7 = 21$	$3 \times 8 = 24$	$3 \times 9 = 27$	$3 \times 10 = 30$
$4 \times 6 = 24$	$4 \times 7 = 28$	$4 \times 8 = 32$	$4 \times 9 = 36$	$4 \times 10 = 40$
$5 \times 6 = 30$	$5 \times 7 = 35$	$5 \times 8 = 40$	$5 \times 9 = 45$	$5 \times 10 = 50$
$6 \times 6 = 36$	$6 \times 7 = 42$	$6 \times 8 = 48$	$6 \times 9 = 54$	$6 \times 10 = 60$
$7 \times 6 = 42$	$7 \times 7 = 49$	$7 \times 8 = 56$	$7 \times 9 = 63$	$7 \times 10 = 70$
$8 \times 6 = 48$	$8 \times 7 = 56$	$8 \times 8 = 64$	$8 \times 9 = 72$	$8 \times 10 = 80$
$9 \times 6 = 54$	$9 \times 7 = 63$	$9 \times 8 = 72$	$9 \times 9 = 81$	$9 \times 10 = 90$
$10 \times 6 = 60$	$10 \times 7 = 70$	$10 \times 8 = 80$	$10 \times 9 = 90$	$10 \times 10 = 100$

Go back and look at the array of numbers on the grid.
Do the patterns make sense?

2x2=4

2
2

HERSHEY'S   HERSHEY'S

HERSHEY'S   HERSHEY'S

Forget about the math for a second. Look at the mosaic.
When you create a picture using small pieces of stone, wood, tile,
or glass it is called a mosaic. Oh, yeah! Two times two equals four.

$$2 \times 3 = 6$$

Two times three equals six. While reading this book, think about your favorite type of art. Is it oil paints? What type of arithmetic is your favorite? Is it multiplication, addition, subtraction, or division?

2 × 4 = 8

Multiplication is a quick way to add equal numbers.
Two times four is the same as two plus two plus two plus two. They both equal eight.
The kids are covered with soot because it is fun but messy to draw with charcoal.

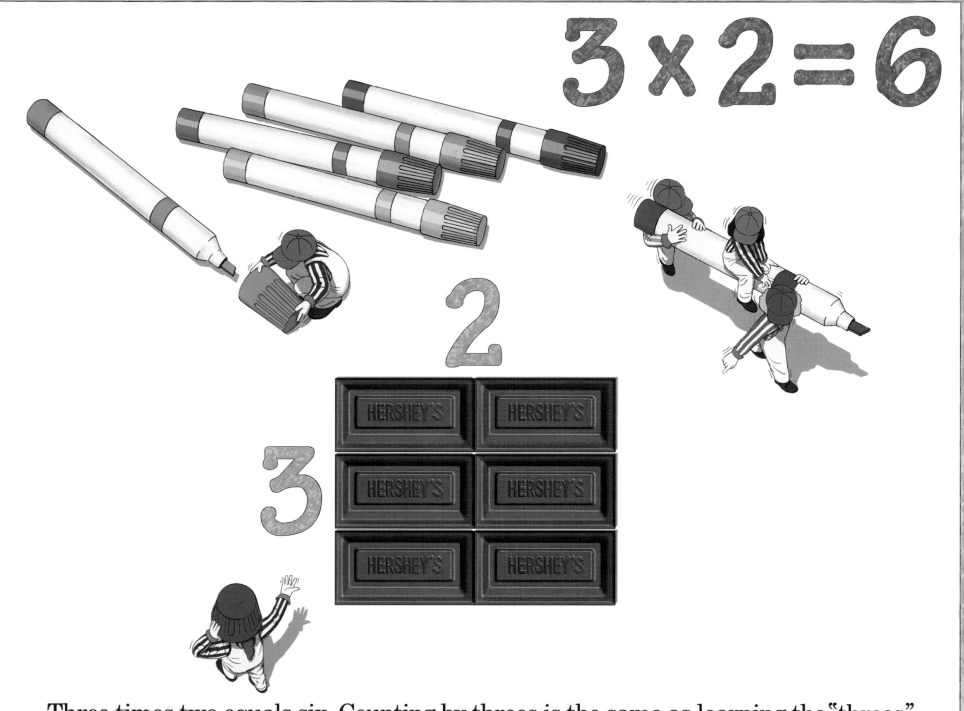

$3 \times 2 = 6$

Three times two equals six. Counting by threes is the same as learning the "threes" multiplication table. Three, six, nine, twelve, fifteen, eighteen, twenty-one, twenty-four, twenty-seven, thirty—keep on counting while drawing with the markers.

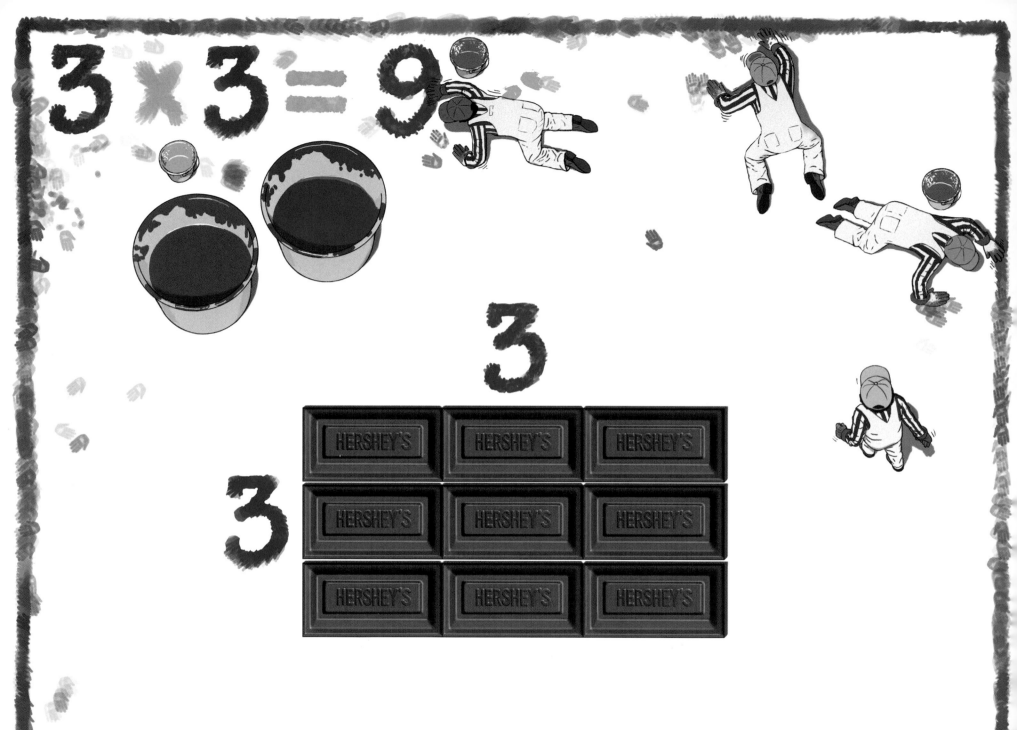

When a number is multiplied by itself, the product is called a square number. Three times three equals nine. When you draw or paint using your hands and fingers as brushes, it is called finger painting. Do not lick your fingers!

SQUARE NUMBERS

The HERSHEY'S milk chocolate bar is shaped like a rectangle, but the answers shown below are square numbers.

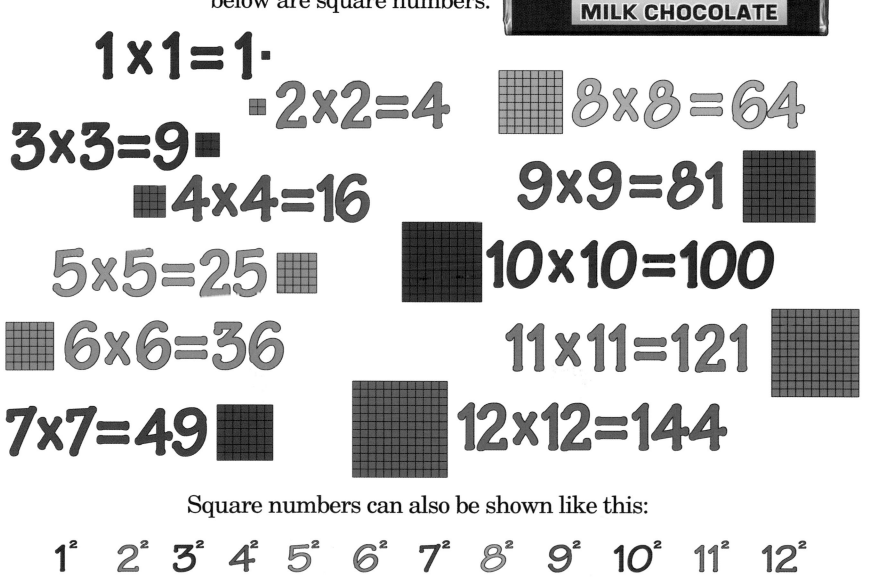

1 x 1 = 1

2 x 2 = 4

8 x 8 = 64

3 x 3 = 9

4 x 4 = 16

9 x 9 = 81

5 x 5 = 25

10 x 10 = 100

6 x 6 = 36

11 x 11 = 121

7 x 7 = 49

12 x 12 = 144

Square numbers can also be shown like this:

1^2 2^2 3^2 4^2 5^2 6^2 7^2 8^2 9^2 10^2 11^2 12^2

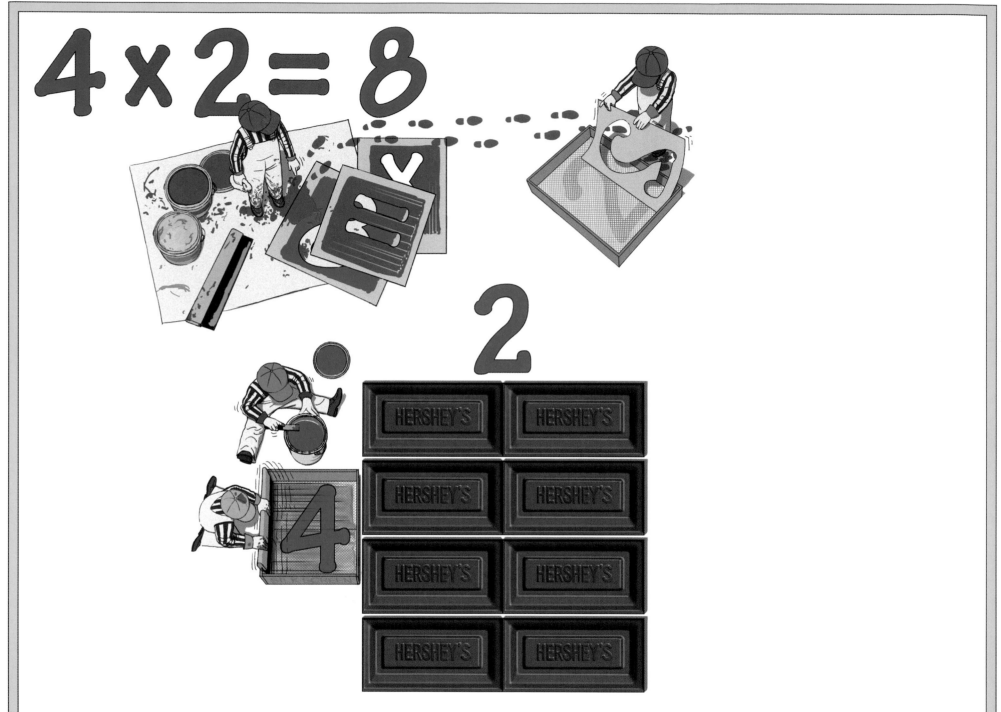

Four times two equals eight. If you want to be really technical,
the first factor is called the multiplicand, and the second factor is called the multiplier.
The kids are silk-screening. They squeegee ink through the cloth to print the numbers.

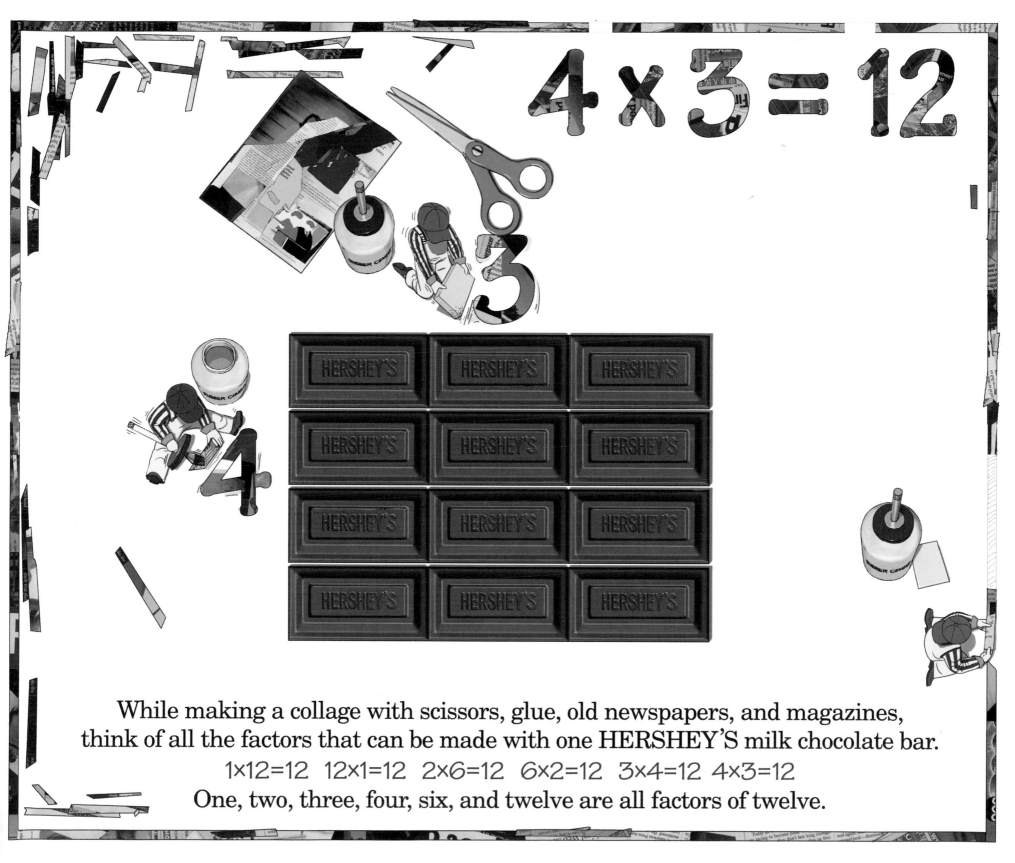

$4 \times 3 = 12$

While making a collage with scissors, glue, old newspapers, and magazines, think of all the factors that can be made with one HERSHEY'S milk chocolate bar.

$1 \times 12 = 12$ $12 \times 1 = 12$ $2 \times 6 = 12$ $6 \times 2 = 12$ $3 \times 4 = 12$ $4 \times 3 = 12$

One, two, three, four, six, and twelve are all factors of twelve.

Four times four equals sixteen. Sixteen is a square number. If someone asks you, "What is the square root of sixteen?" the answer is four. You will learn "square roots" in division. Do not be confused by the linoleum cuts.
Ink is applied on the backward design and then printed in reverse!

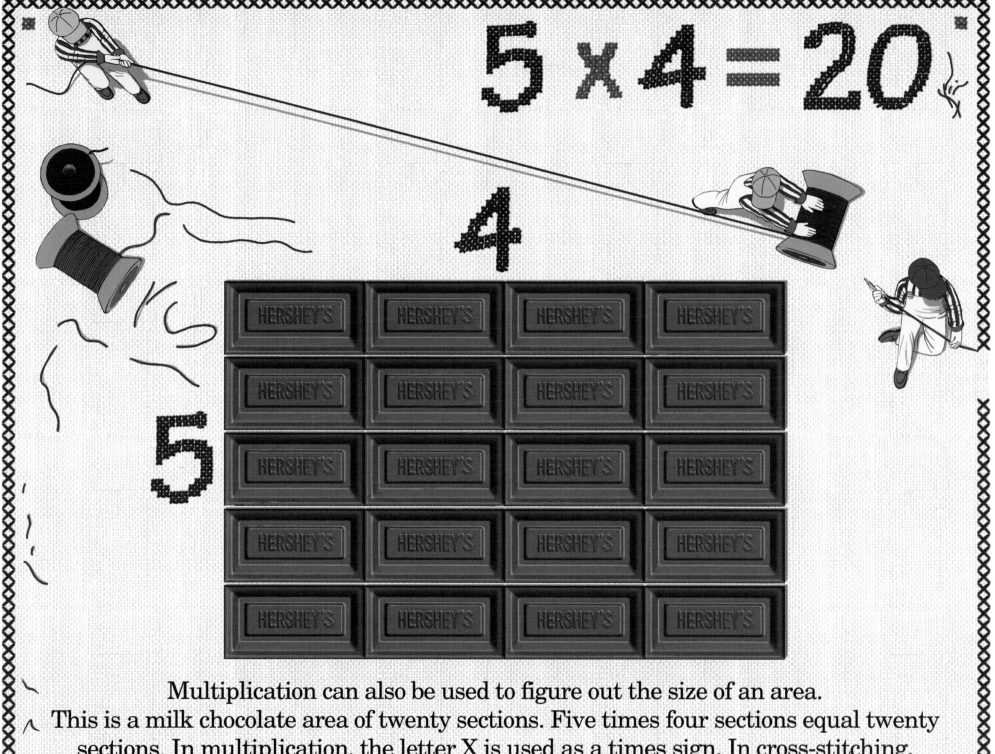

$$5 \times 4 = 20$$

Multiplication can also be used to figure out the size of an area.
This is a milk chocolate area of twenty sections. Five times four sections equal twenty
sections. In multiplication, the letter X is used as a times sign. In cross-stitching,
sewing an X pattern with different colored threads makes a design.

If we take two HERSHEY'S milk chocolate bars and put them next to each other, we now have six times four equals twenty-four. Writing multiplication facts with sidewalk chalk is a great way to practice your math.

2x12=24

After covering the page with pencil, you can draw with erasers. Cool! It is possible to count the sections on the candy bars without taking off the wrappers. You already know that each bar has twelve sections. You can get the answer by doing multiplication. Two times twelve equals twenty-four.

It would take forever to count all the sections in these ten HERSHEY'S bars. Ten times twelve equals one hundred and twenty. Multiplication makes it easy. Tap. Tap. Tap. The kids are hanging up their artwork.

There are 480 sections of chocolate on this page. The associative property of multiplication allows you to do the math two ways. First, try 4 x 10 = 40 and then 40 x 12 = 480. Or do it like this: 4 x the product of 10 x 12. 10 x 12 = 120. 4 x 120 = 480. The answer is the same. Rearrange the mobiles.